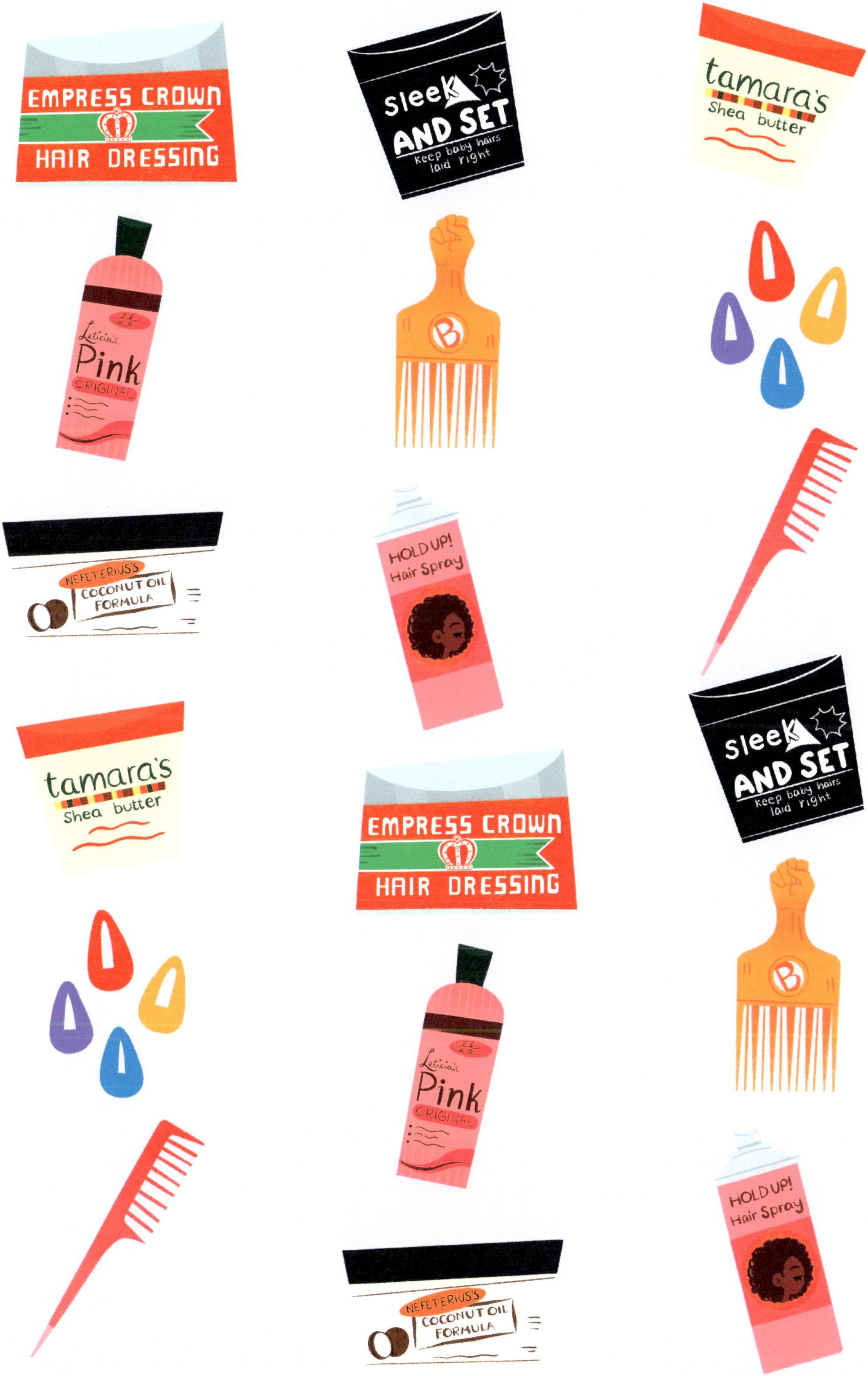
EMPRESS CROWN
HAIR DRESSING
Sleek AND SET
Keep baby hairs laid right
tamara's
Shea butter
Leticia's
Pink
ORIGINAL
B
NEFETERIUS'S
COCONUT OIL FORMULA
HOLD UP!
Hair Spray

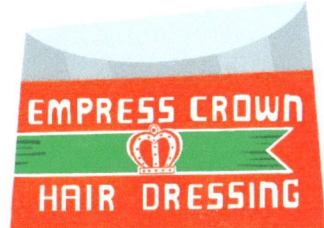

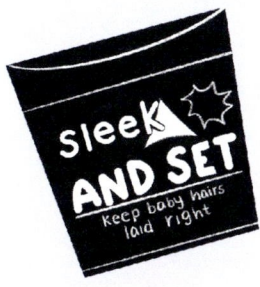

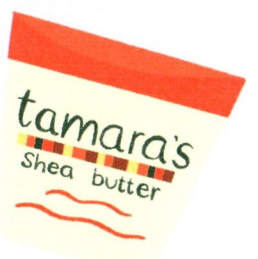

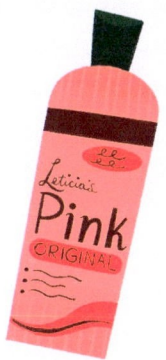

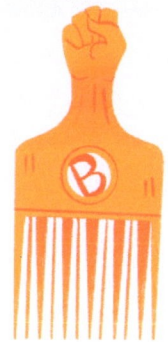

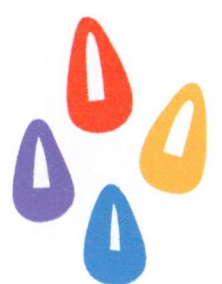

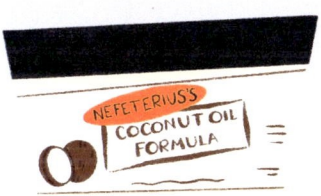

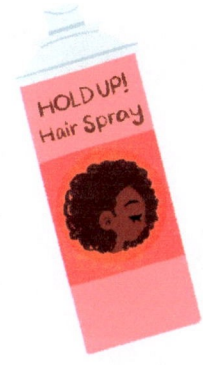

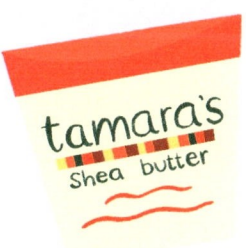

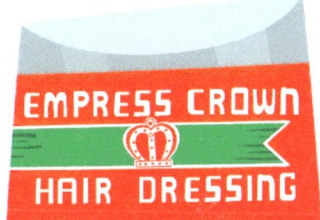

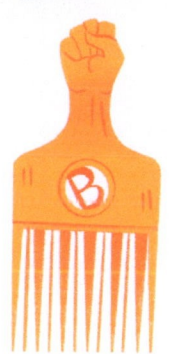

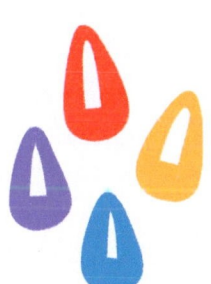

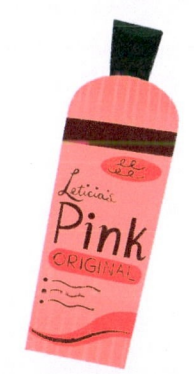

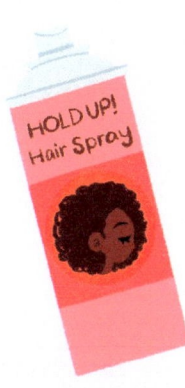

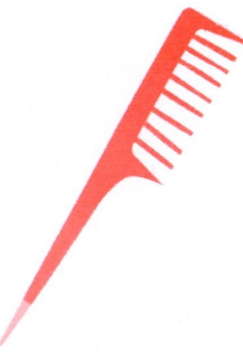

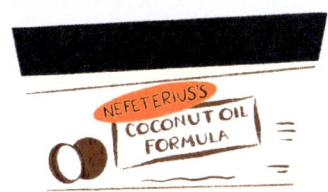

For my curly whirlies: Noah, Milo, Zen and Lotus and for my mom Katharyn and my sister Nefeterius - T.P.

www.theenglishschoolhouse.com

Text copyright © 2020 by Tamara Pizzoli

Pictures copyright © 2020 by Anna Angrick

All rights reserved.

This book or any portion thereof may not be reproduced or used in any manner whatsoever without the express written permission of the author except for the use of brief quotations in a book review. This is a work of fiction. Names, characters, places, and incidents are a product of the author's imagination. Any resemblance to actual persons, events, or locales is entirely coincidental.

ISBN: 978-0-9992108-8-8

Harriet Hare the Hair Guru

Written by Dr. Tamara Pizzoli

Illustrated by Anna Angrick

THE ENGLISH SCHOOL HOUSE

Harriet Hare had shown a talent for doing hair for as long as she or anyone she knew could remember. While most kids her age were mastering sorting and spelling, Harriet was up to her eyebrows in books and magazines featuring cuts, curls, and comb-overs.

"She gets it from me," Harriet's father boasted to his friends.

"It's because of all the time she spends in my barbershop, Hare's Hair Salon."

"No, that's not it," Harriet's mother interjected.

"Harriet's just naturally head honcho when it comes to hairdos."

Harriet's best friends, Zainab and Amir nodded in agreement. Neither of them had ever been to a professional hairstylist or barber. Harriet always had their hair handled, especially on festive occasions and holidays.

During recess, while the other students played hopscotch, Harriet had a line of repeat customers patiently waiting for their hair makeovers. Instead of a ball or sidewalk chalk, Harriet brought her homemade Hold Up hair spray, gels, and pomades to ensure her styles stood up to the test of hard playing.

Soon Harriet began taking after-school appointments outside her father's shop. One client who'd come in happened to be a journalist for Twist and Shout Hair Magazine and featured Harriet on their website. The very next day, a music legend and icon waltzed into Hare's Hair Salon and requested that Harriet trim his Afro to perfection. Harriet's hair services were soon in high demand.

Harriet was officially in business by herself, for herself. Seemingly overnight, her establishment got a major upgrade. The waiting list was more than a year to book an appointment with Ms. Harriet.

Harriet posted her favorite hair creations daily on her Hold Up Flexstagram account, which had reached more than a million followers.

Zainab and Amir were ecstatic about Harriet's newfound success but a bit frustrated by her lack of availability.
"I went to the barber for the first time ever last week," lamented Amir. "Our uncle got married and your mom said you were working every time we stopped by."
"I wore my hijab to the wedding, so that worked," Zainab said.

Along with fame came fans and fun, but also fallouts. Harriet knew things were different when one day after school, she was bombarded by a crowd of personal assistants. It was the first time since kindergarten that she didn't walk home with Zainab and Amir. That evening, she stopped by her best friends' home and rang the doorbell. There was no answer.

Harriet!!

Days later, Harriet received an invitation to the exclusive annual SET Gala in Los Angeles, California, on the firsl Monday in May.

Though Harriet was able to keep up with the intense professional demands of being a hair guru, she began to feel as though something was ... well, missing.

The next day, Harriet's parents and her new assistant sat in the living room, planning what she'd been most looking forward to all year: summer vacation. The plans, however, didn't sound at all like what she had in mind. Instead of late summer nights and water-balloon fights with friends and Popsicle parties, they were discussing budgets, proposals, and branding. Just when they asked Harriet for her opinion, she heard shrieks of laughter and splashes coming from nearby.

Harriet followed the sounds to Zainab's and Amir's home and walked inside the wide-open door. There was a party going on. Harriet's heart sank. She hadn't even been invited to her best friends' party.

She'd almost reached the door when two small hands grabbed her shoulders. "We can't believe you made it!" they shrieked.

"What?" Harriet mumbled, wiping away a tear. "I wasn't invited."

"We dropped by last week to give the invite to you in person," Amir began, "but you were working. So we just left the invitation on your desk."

Harriet smiled, and they all danced and jumped and sang and ate until long after the sun had gone down.

Later that night, Harriet told her parents the truth.
"I miss the times when I could do hair without all the pressure and tight schedules and appearances. I miss my friends and parties and fun. I miss things the way they were."
Harriet's mother smiled and gently stroked her daughter's forehead. Her dad scooped her up and held her in the tightest bear hug.

Her dad spoke first: "Harriet, you must always remember to simply ask for what you need."
Harriet thought a moment ...

and then the answer came to her.
"I need the best of both worlds."

The next morning, the phone rang. Harriet's mother shouted, "Former President Barack Obama is on the phone calling to have Harriet participate as a fellow in his new initiative for young entrepreneurs!"

Without skipping a beat, Harriet replied, "Ask him if Tuesday works, please. Monday I've got a spelling test, Wednesday I have dance class, and I'm not missing the pajama party on Friday. Just have his people call my people."

EMPRESS CROWN
HAIR DRESSING
sleek AND SET
keep baby hairs laid right
tamara's
Shea butter
Leticia's
Pink
ORIGINAL
HOLD UP!
Hair Spray
NEFETERIUS'S
COCONUT OIL
FORMULA

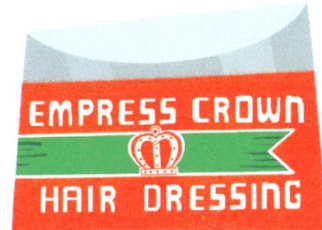

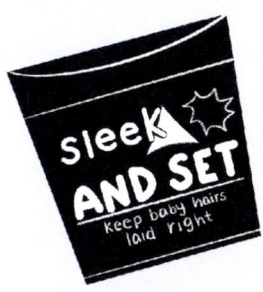

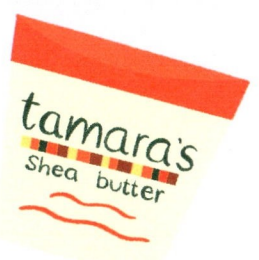

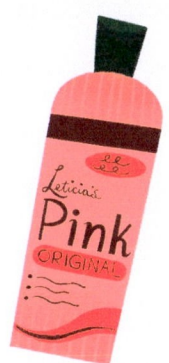

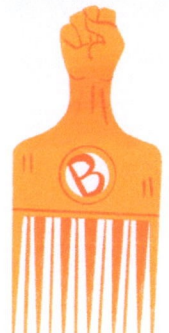

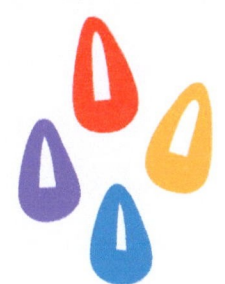

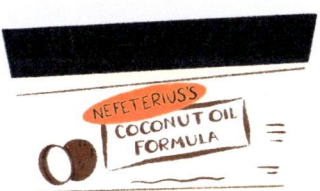

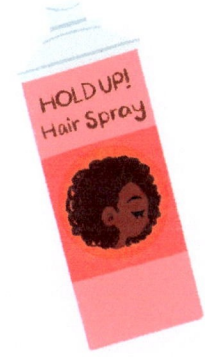

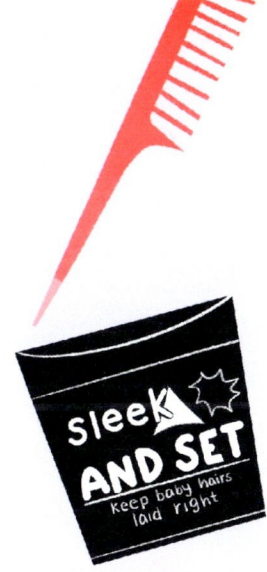

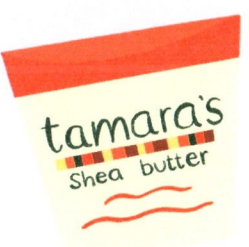

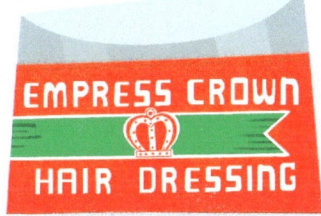

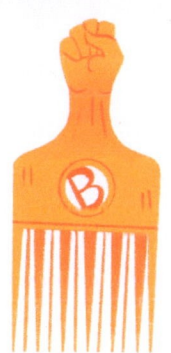

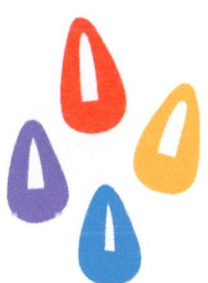

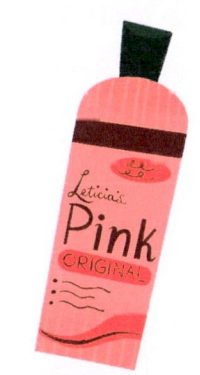

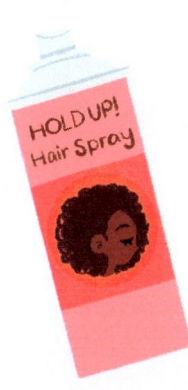

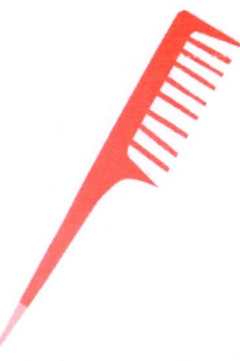

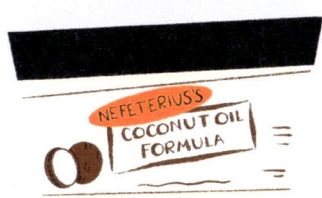

Made in the USA
Columbia, SC
08 April 2025